Eight Short Preludes
on Gregorian Themes
for Organ
Opus 45

by
MARCEL DUPRÉ

CONTENTS

Page

SALVE REGINA
Opus 45, No. 1

MARCEL DUPRÉ

Foundations 16', 4'

Summy-Birchard Inc. exclusively distributed by
Alfred Music

VIRGO DEI GENITRIX

Opus 45, No. 2

Tutti

8va

PANGE LINGUA
(Tantum Ergo)
Opus 45, No. 3

Flute 8'

SACRIS SOLEMNIIS

(Panis Angelicus)
Opus 45, No. 4

Foundations 8', 4'

ALMA REDEMPTORIS MATER
Opus 45, No. 5

I: Dulciana 8'
II: Cornet

AVE VERUM CORPUS
Opus 45, No. 6

I: Salicional 8'
II: Voix Celeste 8'

LAUDA SION
(Ecce Panis)
Opus 45, No. 7

Foundations 8', 4', Mixtures

VERBUM SUPERNUM
(O Salutaris)
Opus 45, No. 8